You could go off and play all day where Floyd lived.

There was a field for racing and chasing games, which were his favourite. And up the hill was the tree with a tyre, which was his other favourite. The only place you weren't allowed to go was down in the valley behind the houses...

Floyd's house

The tree   The field

For Rafabear – S.T. For Ben and Lucy – N.L.
First published 2015 by Walker Books Ltd, 87 Vauxhall
Walk, London SE11 5HJ • 10 9 8 7 6 5 4 3 2 1 • Text © 2015
Sean Taylor • Illustrations © 2015 Neal Layton • The right
of Sean Taylor and Neal Layton to be identified as author and illustrator respectively
of this work has been asserted by them in accordance with the Copyright, Designs and
Patents Act 1988 • This book has been typeset in Layton, Joanna and Franklin Gothic

WALKER BOOKS
AND SUBSIDIARIES
LONDON • BOSTON • SYDNEY • AUCKLAND

Condensed • Printed in China • All rights reserved. No part
of this book may be reproduced, transmitted or stored in an
information retrieval system in any form or by any means,
graphic, electronic or mechanical, including photocopying,
taping and recording, without prior written permission from the publisher. •
British Library Cataloguing in Publication Data: a catalogue record for this book is
available from the British Library • ISBN 978-1-4063-2414-3 • www.walker.co.uk

WHERE THE BUGABOO LIVES

SEAN TAYLOR • illustrated by NEAL LAYTON

The valley

"Why can't we go down in the valley behind the houses?" Floyd asked.

His mum looked at him for a moment. Then she said, "It's all dark and shadowy down there and it wouldn't be any fun for playing."

But Floyd asked his sister, Ruby, the same question and she said something different.

"If I tell you," she said, "YOU MIGHT NOT BE ABLE TO GO TO SLEEP EVER AGAIN!"

"I *will* be able to," nodded Floyd. So Ruby *did* tell him.

She said, "We can't go into the valley because scary things live there. And the scariest of all is **THE BUGABOO**."

Floyd did go to sleep that night. But he dreamt about

THE BUGABOO.

And he didn't want to go into the valley the next day. It was only because of the ball. It was the best ball he'd ever had. He felt sadder and sadder as it rolled away.

"Can't we ever go and get it from the valley?" he asked.

"You're too young to go down there where the scary things live," said Ruby.

"But I'm the oldest I've ever been," said Floyd. "And if we creep quietly as mice, **THE BUGABOO** will never know."

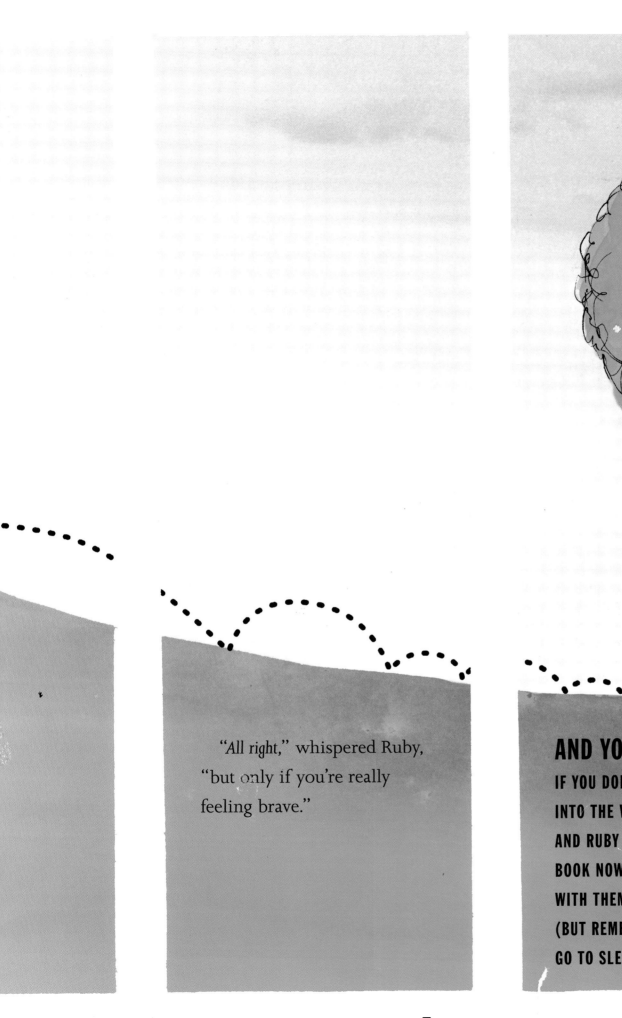

"All right," whispered Ruby, "but only if you're really feeling brave."

AND YOU CAN CHOOSE. IF YOU DON'T WANT TO GO DOWN INTO THE VALLEY WITH FLOYD AND RUBY ... THEN SHUT THE BOOK NOW. IF YOU WANT TO GO WITH THEM ... TURN THE PAGE. (BUT REMEMBER, YOU MIGHT NOT GO TO SLEEP EVER AGAIN.)

With each step, the houses got further away and the trees got nearer. Floyd picked up his ball, put it in his pocket and smiled. But Ruby wasn't smiling. She could see six … eight … ten little crocodile ogres with teeth as sharp as scissors.

Floyd asked Ruby, "Is there a cupboard we could hide in?" But Ruby shook her head. She had another idea…

YOU LOT COULDN'T GET US! YOU COULDN'T EVEN SAY … *THE BAD BLUE BUG BIT THE BIG BLACK BEAR!*

The crocodile ogres tried to say Ruby's tongue-twister...

THE BAG BOD BID...

BLUH!

THE BAD ... THE BLUE ... THE BLOOD?

BLAH!

BLUH!

BLAH!

BLUH!

And the children took their chance. They ran until they reached a sign. It said, THE START OF THE PATH. They took the path and, a little way along, it led two different ways. The first way went uphill. The second way went downhill.

AND YOU CAN CHOOSE.

IF YOU WANT FLOYD AND RUBY TO GO UPHILL ... THEN TURN THE PAGE. IF YOU WANT THEM TO GO DOWNHILL ... THEN TURN TO PAGE 14.

FLOYD AND RUBY TOOK THE UPHILL PATH.
The tall trees watched as they hurried on. But ahead was a swarm of great big mosquitoes with horribly long prongs. They zoomed at the children. Floyd and Ruby flapped and ducked, but there was no getting away from them.

One of them buzzed, "We're going to suck blood from your hearts! From your hearts!"

"Yes we are," hummed another.

"The blood from your hearts!"

"Do you think there's a shop where we can buy some bug spray?" whispered Floyd.

But Ruby had another idea. "Sorry," she said, "we didn't bring our hearts with us today."

"What?" droned the mosquitoes.

"We didn't bring our hearts with us," repeated Ruby, "but we'll go and get them if you want, and come straight back."

The mosquitoes didn't look happy.

"Will you *really*?" one of them buzzed. Ruby nodded and the mosquitoes zig-zagged out of their way.

So Floyd and Ruby hurried off as fast as they dared.

The path ahead split in two. One way it looked as if it was spring. The other way it looked as if it was autumn.

AND YOU CAN CHOOSE.

IF YOU WANT FLOYD AND RUBY TO TAKE THE SPRING PATH … THEN TURN TO PAGE 16. IF YOU WANT THEM TO TAKE THE AUTUMN PATH … THEN TURN TO PAGE 18.

FLOYD AND RUBY TOOK THE DOWNHILL PATH.
Trees closed in around them and they reached a place where there were flowers on both sides of the path. And the flowers slowly turned, as if they were looking at the children. Floyd and Ruby felt strangely sleepy. Ruby yawned.

Floyd said, "I think I'm going to lie down."

As he spoke, stalks snaked towards his nose and voices whispered, "Don't we smell lovely?"

"DON'T SNIFF THEM!" said Ruby. "THE SMELL IS SENDING YOU TO SLEEP AND THE BUGABOO WILL GET US!"

But the flowers had almost blocked the path.

"I think we need to find a tractor and drive through on it," said Floyd. But Ruby had another idea.

14

"Sorry," she said. "We've both got really bad colds, so we can't smell anything." The flowers stopped moving and looked at each other as if they didn't know what to do. The children took their chance and ran.

The path ahead split in two. In one direction, it looked as if it was winter. In the other, it looked as if it was summer.

AND YOU CAN CHOOSE. IF YOU WANT FLOYD AND RUBY TO TAKE THE WINTER PATH … THEN TURN TO PAGE 20. IF YOU WANT THEM TO TAKE THE SUMMER PATH … THEN TURN TO PAGE 22.

15

THE CHILDREN CHOSE THE SPRING PATH.

As they hurried along, they passed bits of broken toys. And then they stopped. Ahead, in a sandpit, was a giant little girl. She threw down a doll and waddled towards them.

"You can be my new toys!" she smiled.

Floyd swallowed and whispered, "Maybe we should say we've got a bus to catch, so we haven't got time to play?"

But that wasn't what Ruby was thinking. "Look over there, there's a man giving away ice-creams!"

"Ice-creams?" asked the girl. And she toddled to where Ruby was pointing. Ruby grabbed Floyd's hand and they ran on.

16

"I'm not in the mood for ever meeting her again!" said Floyd.

"I'm not in the mood for meeting **THE BUGABOO**," Ruby told him.

Ahead the path split in two. One way, the air was full of smoke.

The other way was lit up by coloured lights.

WHICH WAY DO YOU WANT FLOYD AND RUBY TO GO THIS TIME?

IF YOU WANT THEM TO HEAD FOR THE SMOKE … THEN TURN TO PAGE 24.

IF YOU WANT THEM TO HEAD FOR THE COLOURED LIGHTS … TURN TO PAGE 26.

THE CHILDREN CHOSE THE AUTUMN PATH.
Nothing moved but leaves in the breeze. Then they saw it! A weaselly werewolf crouching in the shadows.

18

"Maybe the best thing is if we pretend we're actually already dead," whispered Floyd.

Then the werewolf pounced so close they could feel its hot breath.

"GOTCHA!" it snarled.

But Ruby said, "I don't think so, because lots of wolf hunters are right behind us."

The werewolf twitched its hairy snout.

"Wolf hunters?" it growled.

"With big wolf-hunting weapons," nodded Floyd.

The werewolf gave a frightened blink. Then he slunk out of sight.

Ruby grabbed Floyd's hand and they dashed on.

"I wish I'd brought my bicycle helmet," said Floyd.

"You'll need more than a bicycle helmet if we meet **THE BUGABOO**," Ruby told him.

And ahead of them, the path split in two. One way smelt of honey. The other way smelt of dustbins.

WHICH WAY DO YOU WANT FLOYD AND RUBY TO GO THIS TIME? IF YOU WANT THEM TO GO THE WAY THAT SMELLS OF HONEY ... THEN TURN TO PAGE 28. IF YOU WANT THEM TO GO THE WAY THAT SMELLS OF DUSTBINS ... TURN TO PAGE 30.

THE CHILDREN CHOSE THE WINTER PATH. It led through a jumble of brambly bushes. They hadn't gone far when they found an unbelievably horrible spiky thing was blocking the way.

"You chose the wrong path!" it blurted out. "I'm a long-nosed prickle beast and NOBODY GETS PAST ME!"

Floyd stared at the prickles as sharp as pins, and asked, "Can we call the fire brigade?"

But that wasn't what Ruby was thinking. "Run!" she whispered. "Run through its legs!"

She ducked. Floyd dived after. Lightning seemed to fill the prickle beast's eyes. It blinked and snagged on brambles, as it tried to turn. But the children were already away along the path.

"That was a near shave!" said Floyd, looking back.

"That wasn't anything compared to if we meet **THE BUGABOO**…" said Ruby.

And ahead of them the path split in two. One way, there were neat hedges and statues. The other way, everything was messy and smashed.

WHICH WAY DO YOU WANT FLOYD AND RUBY TO GO THIS TIME?

IF YOU WANT THEM TO TAKE THE NEAT PATH … THEN TURN TO PAGE 32. IF YOU WANT THEM TO TAKE THE MESSY PATH … TURN TO PAGE 34.

21

THE CHILDREN CHOSE THE SUMMER PATH.

It led to a rickety bridge over a river.
And before they had taken two steps
across, a sour-faced troll swung himself
up. He stamped his foot and bellowed:

THIS IS MY BRIDGE!
TRY TO CROSS AND I'LL TOSS
YOU IN THE RIVER!

Floyd blinked
and whispered,
"I think we need
one of those
tranquilizer guns
that zookeepers use
to send elephants
to sleep."

But that wasn't
what Ruby was
thinking. She
picked up a stick
and threw it.
Then she shouted,
"FETCH!"

The River

22

The troll watched the stick land, then bounced away to fetch it. Ruby took Floyd's hand. They ran over the bridge and darted on into the shadows.

"That didn't actually frighten me," said Floyd.

"Good," nodded Ruby, "because you're going to need to be extra brave if we meet **THE BUGABOO**."

Ahead the path split in two. Coming from one way, was a sound of croaking frogs. From the other, there was a sound of funky music.

WHICH WAY DO YOU WANT FLOYD AND RUBY TO GO THIS TIME?

IF YOU WANT THEM TO HEAD FOR THE FROGS ... THEN TURN TO PAGE 36. IF YOU WANT THEM TO HEAD FOR THE FUNKY MUSIC ... TURN TO PAGE 38.

THEY WALKED INTO THE SMOKE. The air grew hotter with each step. Gusts of sparks billowed past. And there, in a pit full of fire, was a burning fiend. Each breath wheezed in his lungs as he lurched towards them. When he stopped, he hissed:

It's not safe to go any further. That's where **THE BUGABOO** lives. But you're not safe here either, BECAUSE I'LL DRAG YOU INTO MY PIT AND BARBEQUE YOU, THEN EAT YOU UP WITH TOMATO KETCHUP!

Floyd said,
I KNOW, LET'S TELL HIM OUR MUM SAYS IT'S NOT GOOD MANNERS TO BARBEQUE PEOPLE.

But Ruby shook her head. As the fiend reached out his long fingers, she quickly said, "Watch out! It looks as if it's going to start raining!"

The fiend hesitated. Then he looked up at the sky. Floyd and Ruby ran.

AND THIS TIME THERE WAS ONLY ONE WAY AHEAD.
THERE WAS NO GOING BACK THE WAY THEY HAD COME. AND THERE'S NO GOING BACK FOR YOU.
THE ONLY THING IS TO TURN TO PAGE 40.

THEY WALKED TOWARDS THE COLOURED LIGHTS.

And out popped a freaky flibbertigibbet.

"Go any further and you'll end up where **THE BUGABOO** lives," he grinned. "But I'll save you the trouble, because I've got more than twenty horrible ways to catch you!"

"Maybe we can tell him we're actually horrible monsters ourselves," whispered Floyd.

The freaky flibbertigibbet gave a giggle and his hat fell off.

"I'll get you, whatever
ideas you have!" he called out. "If I
touch this super-twang elastic, you'll
be pinged into a net. If I toggle this nozzle-
pumper, a whizz-whirring scoop-you-up will sweep you
off your feet. And if I whojamaflick this whojamaflip, you'll
drop like stones into a trap-hole that nobody can see!"

He put his hat back on but, as he did, Ruby pulled it over his
eyes. Then she and Floyd ran. And, from behind them, there
was a clunk as the freaky flibbertigibbet fell into the trap-hole
that nobody could see.

AND THIS TIME THERE WAS ONLY ONE WAY AHEAD.

THERE WAS NO GOING BACK THE WAY THEY HAD COME. AND THERE'S NO GOING
BACK FOR YOU. THE ONLY THING IS TO TURN TO PAGE 40.

THEY TOOK THE WAY THAT SMELT OF HONEY.

And there was a witch, looking at them with eyes as cold as marbles.

The witch came towards them with a plastic sack. "Now, my little pumpernickels!" she smiled. "This path leads to where **THE BUGABOO** lives. So I suggest you stay here and have a rest in my sack. You'll find toffees and liquorice-suckers inside."

Floyd shook his head and said, "Our mum told us never to take sweets from strange old people."

The witch's expression changed…

28

She said,
GET IN MY SACK!
Or I'll turn you
into a pair of
burger buns!

But Ruby called out,
YOU CAN'T ACTUALLY
TURN US INTO
BURGER BUNS!

The witch tutted,
I can! I can
turn anything
into anything!

So Ruby said,
THEN TURN YOURSELF
INTO ... A TEASPOON.

The witch said a spell.
In a flash ...

she was a teaspoon.

Ruby picked it up, dropped it
into the sack and tied it up.

Then they hurried on.

**AND THIS TIME
THERE WAS ONLY
ONE WAY AHEAD.**
THERE WAS NO GOING BACK
THE WAY THEY HAD COME.
AND THERE'S NO GOING BACK
FOR YOU. THE ONLY THING IS
TO TURN TO PAGE 40.

THEY WALKED ON AND SOON FOUND
OUT WHERE THE SMELL WAS COMING FROM.

Ahead was a rubbish heap. On top
was a gigantic spider. Floyd and
Ruby froze … but the spider had
seen them and came scuttling over.
The children only had a moment.
They hid, but the spider's feathery
footsteps were getting nearer
and a soft voice said:

AND THIS TIME THERE
WAS ONLY ONE WAY AHEAD.

THERE WAS NO GOING BACK THE WAY THEY HAD
COME. AND THERE'S NO GOING BACK FOR YOU.
THE ONLY THING IS TO TURN TO PAGE 40.

It landed with a rattle and the spider
scuttled after, thinking she had found them.
But Floyd and Ruby were actually off and
away down the path.

Don't go any
further. You're heading
for where here, and
lives. Stay the THE BUGABOO
Let me squeeze the
juice out of you!

"Perhaps we can frighten her
away if we both shout BOO very
suddenly?" Floyd whispered.
But Ruby had another idea. She
picked up a bottle top and threw
it as far as she could.

THE COUNTRY RESIDENCE OF

The Old English Spook

(Keep out!)

AHEAD WAS A GREAT, GRAND HOUSE. And out came the Old English Spook.

"Deary me!" he called down the steps.

"Trespassing children! What shall I do?"

He fixed them with piercing eyes.

"I mustn't let you go on because you're heading for where **THE BUGABOO** lives. No, I have a better idea. I'll tell my cook to chop you up and make me a nice boy-girl curry!"

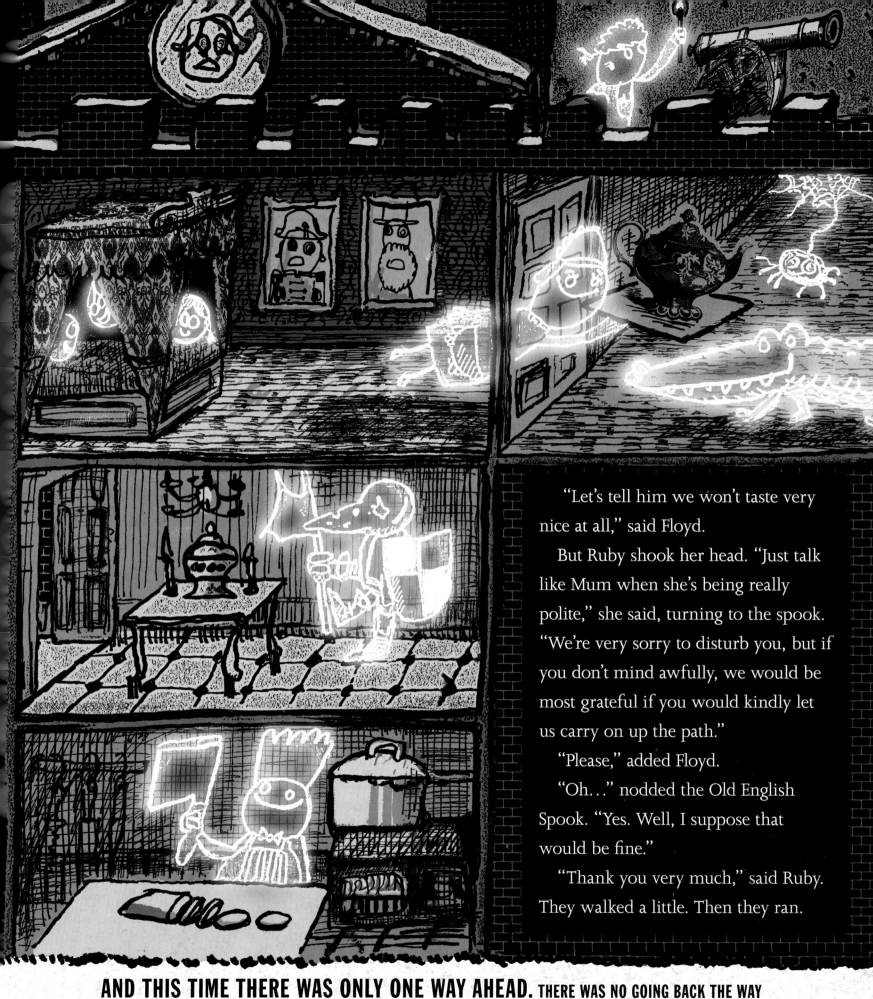

"Let's tell him we won't taste very nice at all," said Floyd.

But Ruby shook her head. "Just talk like Mum when she's being really polite," she said, turning to the spook. "We're very sorry to disturb you, but if you don't mind awfully, we would be most grateful if you would kindly let us carry on up the path."

"Please," added Floyd.

"Oh…" nodded the Old English Spook. "Yes. Well, I suppose that would be fine."

"Thank you very much," said Ruby. They walked a little. Then they ran.

AND THIS TIME THERE WAS ONLY ONE WAY AHEAD. THERE WAS NO GOING BACK THE WAY THEY HAD COME. AND THERE'S NO GOING BACK FOR YOU. THE ONLY THING IS TO TURN TO PAGE 40.

THEY WALKED BETWEEN SMASHED ROCKS AND UPTURNED TREE TRUNKS.

It was very quiet. Then, suddenly, there was a thunder of boots and out bounded a

bony hobgoblin, bellowing with laughter from its knobbly nose to its hobbly knees.

"You're in trouble now, LITTLE BRATS! Keep going and you'll meet **THE BUGABOO**!

Stay here and I'll BREAK YOUR BONES LIKE BISCUITS!"

"Let's say we're wearing bullet-proof vests," whispered Floyd.

But Ruby shook her head. As the hobgoblin raised its club,

she reached down and quickly tied together its boot laces.

Then she shouted, "Run!"

The hobgoblin lashed and lunged and tried to follow.

But, because its boots were tied together, it toppled with a

thud that made the ground shake. And Floyd and Ruby ran on.

THIS TIME THERE WAS ONLY ONE WAY AHEAD. THERE WAS NO GOING BACK THE

WAY THEY HAD COME. AND THERE'S NO GOING BACK FOR YOU. THE ONLY THING IS TO TURN TO PAGE 40.

THEY WALKED TOWARDS THE SOUND OF CROAKING FROGS, AND FOUND THEMSELVES CROSSING A SWAMP.

On the far side was an old gate, and a drooling demon's head slurped out of the slime. It opened its mouth in a sticky smile and a frog jumped out.

The demon drooled,
This gate is locked to keep THE BUGABOO out. And if you want the key, you'll have to jump in here to find it.

Floyd asked,
WHY DON'T WE SAY OUR MUM FOUND OUT WE'RE BOTH ALLERGIC TO SLIME?

Ruby shook her head and said to the demon,

I DON'T BELIEVE YOU. YOU CAN'T KEEP THE KEY DOWN THERE.

I CAN! LOOK!

The demon splooshed down and came up with the key.

Ruby snatched it. The demon groaned,

NO!

But she was already opening the gate. Then she and Floyd were through.

AND THIS TIME THERE WAS ONLY ONE WAY AHEAD.

THERE WAS NO GOING BACK THE WAY THEY HAD COME. AND THERE'S NO GOING BACK FOR YOU. THE ONLY THING IS TO TURN TO PAGE 40.

THEY WALKED TOWARDS THE SOUND OF FUNKY MUSIC.
And a ghastly figure came gliding towards them like an icy breeze.

"Can't we walk past and pretend we haven't actually noticed it?" whispered Floyd.

"No," said Ruby. "It's noticed us."

"They call me the cool ghoul," said the figure. "And I wouldn't go down this little path, kiddos. It leads right to **THE BUGABOO**. Stay and check out my spooky party instead."

He pointed to where the music was coming from. There were dozens of other ghosts dancing and beckoning. The children tried to get past, but the cool ghoul blocked the way.

"Tickle it!" Ruby whispered. "Tickle it on its knees and its toes!"

They did and the ghoul burst out laughing. "No!" it gasped. "Please!" Then it collapsed in a heap of wriggling and giggling.

Floyd and Ruby were round it and off…

AND THIS TIME THERE WAS ONLY ONE WAY AHEAD.

THERE WAS NO GOING BACK THE WAY THEY HAD COME. AND THERE'S NO GOING BACK FOR YOU. THE ONLY THING IS TO TURN TO PAGE 40.

The children's footsteps rang through the trees as they raced on, and Floyd called out, "Look!"

Ahead, they could see the tree with the tyre.

"That's the way home!" nodded Ruby. And they ran faster. But not for long.

Because the path came to a cave. And there was …

SPIKY
← HORNS

LOTS OF
EYES

LOTS
AND
LOTS
OF
SHARP
TEETH

SPIKY
TAIL

HORRIBLE
SCALY
SKIN

42

THE BUGABOO!

There has never been a worse monster in any book.

The children stopped as still as birds.

LOTS OF CLAWS

AND YOU CAN CHOOSE.
IF YOU <u>REALLY</u> CAN'T FACE WHAT'S GOING TO HAPPEN NEXT, GO BACK TO THE START OF THE PATH ON PAGE 11. IF YOU'RE BRAVE ENOUGH TO CARRY ON, **TURN THE PAGE...**

Ruby and Floyd tried to hide behind the bushes but **THE BUGABOO** let out a roar so loud it blew the bushes clean out of the ground.

Then he pulled a face so scary that Floyd and Ruby fell flat on their backs.

Then he stamped
his foot so hard, they
bounced back up again.

"I'm thinking of an idea," whispered Floyd.
"Maybe we should get the Bugaboo's mum?"

But Ruby had other ideas. "DON'T EAT US!" she called out. "WE'RE ABSOLUTELY DEADLY POISONOUS!"

THE BUGABOO snatched her into the air and snarled, "I'd be more scared of two clothes pegs!"

Ruby tried again. "Umm... There are some other children coming and they'll be much bigger and tastier than us!"

She hung there, like a coat on a hanger.

"You won't get me with that old trick," said **THE BUGABOO**. And he reached down to grab Floyd too...

But Floyd wasn't there.

THE BUGABOO poked and peered and sniffed. But he couldn't find Floyd. And Ruby didn't know what had happened.

"PLEASE!" she said, "IT'S OUR DINNER TIME! AND I WANT TO GO HOME!"

"I know," said **THE BUGABOO**, "but it's my dinner time! And the more you talk ... THE HUNGRIER I GET!"

But at that very moment, Floyd came out of the cave. And with him was …

THE BUGABOO'S MUM!

THE BUGABOO put Ruby down and looked at the ground.

"Don't start getting all upset," said his mum. "Come here and I'll give you a lovely kiss."

She walked towards **THE BUGABOO**. It was Floyd and Ruby's chance.

AND YOU CAN CHOOSE.

IF YOU'D LIKE TO SEE THE BUGABOO GET A LOVELY KISS, THEN TURN THE PAGE.

IF YOU'D RATHER SKIP THE KISS ...
TURN TO PAGE 52.

Floyd and Ruby ran ...

gasping, stumbling
and grinning ...

out of the valley …

all the way to the tree
with the tyre.

When they arrived back home, their mum said, "You two look as though you've had some fun. What have you been playing?"

"Mainly racing and chasing games," nodded Floyd. "And sometimes we didn't know if we were ever going to get back home."

His mum looked at him for a moment. Then she said, "Well, at least you had Ruby to look after you."

"And she had me to look after her," said Floyd. Then he threw his ball up in the air and caught it.

And that night, Floyd dreamt about everything in the world except for **THE BUGABOO...**

AND THAT <u>IS</u> THE END.

(Unless, of course, you want to go back to the beginning...)